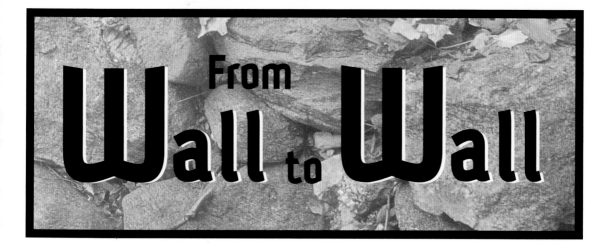

For Bailey

The wall pictured on the cover is *Storm King Wall* by Andy Goldsworthy,
Storm King Art Center, Mountainville, New York.

Changping, China

From Wall to Wall

Susan Kuklin

G. P. Putnam's Sons   New York

We share
w
a
l
l
s.

The Algarve, Portugal

The Dordogne, France

Some are
old and thick
and made
of stone.

Some are
clear and thin
for the sky
to come in.

Chelsea, New York City

Fortress—
barricade—
rampart—
fence.
a wall
can separate
a very large
space.

Mutianyu, China

SoHo, New York City

We share walls.

Walls can
hold back
nature

Southampton, New York

Lucca, Italy

or
provide a
resting
spot.

One does the
h o o t c h y -
k o o t c h y
and walks about
the place.

There are walls
to keep you in.

Ikaruga, Japan

Chelsea, New York City

There are walls
to keep you out.

There's
a
wall
of
silence

and a
place
to
SHOUT.

Harlem, New York City

Montignac-Lascaux, France

Some walls tell a story
about a distant time.

Some show the history of one's hometown.

Crete, Nebraska

Bronx, New York City

Walls can hold our future

and honor friends
from our past.

London, England

Stronghold
—
barrier
—
enclosure
—
shield.

We
share
walls.

AUTHOR'S NOTES

THE ALGARVE, PORTUGAL This photo shows the side of one of the many colorful buildings in southern Portugal.

THE DORDOGNE, FRANCE This wall lines a pathway through a small village. CHELSEA, NEW YORK CITY Artist's installation. Two-Way Mirror Cylinder Inside Cube. Artist: Dan Graham, Rooftop Urban Park Project, Dia Center for the Arts. MUTIANYU, CHINA The Great Wall was built around China to unify the country and keep enemies out. SOHO, NEW YORK CITY Mural. SOUTHAMPTON, NEW YORK These sand castle walls were built by a group of children. Thanks to Stephen Bohlen. LUCCA, ITALY This is the side of a building in a Tuscan town. MOUNTAINVILLE, NEW YORK Artist's installation. *Storm King Wall*. Artist: Andy Goldsworthy, Storm King Art Center. IKARUGA, JAPAN This wall surrounds part of the Horyu Temple complex. CHELSEA, NEW YORK CITY Jasmine Jin from P. S. 11 at the Rooftop Urban Park Project, Dia Center for the Arts. CHELSEA, NEW YORK CITY This wall of silence is made up of P. S. 11 students Aiden Bachtell, Kalon Cheong, Jasmine Jin, Carrosa McAllister, Christopher Oguendo, Jennifer Pichardo, Malik Rushing, and Cecilia Russell. Thanks to teachers Helena Ladowitz, Judy Lorenzo, and Emily Garrick. HARLEM, NEW YORK CITY School yard mural. Artists: P. S. 76 students and muralist William Walsh, with Electra Askitopoulos Friedman of Doing Art Together, Inc.

MONTIGNAC-LASCAUX, FRANCE Walls in the Lascaux caves were painted by Cro-Magnon people. This is a photo of a replica made near the original cave, which was closed for preservation. CRETE, NEBRASKA Mural. Artists: Geoff and Echo Easton and Greg Holdren. Thanks to Reba Kuklin. BRONX, NEW YORK CITY School yard mural. *Living on Mars Mural* © 2000 CITYarts, Inc. Artists: Nils Folke Anderson and Nicky Enright of BIG HANDS; children from New Settlement Youth Program, Jack Doyle, Director, and C. E. S. 64. Director of the Project: Tsipi Ben-Haim. Funders: NASA Art Program and the NASA Astrobiology Institute, NEW SETTLEMENT, American Museum of Natural History, The Universities Space Research Association, The Planetary Society. CHELSEA, NEW YORK CITY Memorial to a pet, West Chelsea Veterinary Hospital. LONDON, ENGLAND The Tower of London was built to defend access to the city from the Thames River. NEW ROCHELLE, NEW YORK This wall was built to define a family's property. Thanks to children Olivia and Frankie Watkins, John Adam Ford, and Bethany Townley; the Butcher/Jackson-Butcher family; and Eve and Beryl Jones-Woodin.

Special thanks to Katherine Hoffman for sharing the Moroccan wedding song, "Ida ou Zeddout."
We are one, me and you, we share walls—our fields share boundaries and springs . . .